D1271485

EDGE
BOOKS™

Forensic Crime Solvers

HANDWRITING EVIDENCE

by Michael Martin

Consultant:
Janis S. Tweedy
Forensic Document Examiner
Mendota Heights, Minnesota

Capstone
press®

Mankato, Minnesota

Edge Books are published by Capstone Press,
151 Good Counsel Drive, P.O. Box 669, Mankato, Minnesota 56002.
www.capstonepress.com

Library of Congress Cataloging-in-Publication Data
Martin, Michael, 1948–
    Handwriting evidence / by Michael Martin.
    p. cm.—(Edge books. Forensic crime solvers)
    Summary: "Describes how handwriting and other document evidence is used to solve
crimes"—Provided by publisher.
    Includes bibliographical references and index.
    ISBN-13: 978-0-7368-6788-7 (hardcover)
    ISBN-10: 0-7368-6788-0 (hardcover)
    ISBN-13: 978-0-7368-7872-2 (softcover pbk.)
    ISBN-10: 0-7368-7872-6 (softcover pbk.)
    1. Writing—Identification—Juvenile literature. 2. Legal documents—
Identification—Juvenile literature. 3. Evidence, Criminal—Juvenile literature. I. Title.
II. Series.
HV8074.M365 2007
363.25'65—dc22   2006024766

Editorial Credits
Angie Kaelberer, editor; Juliette Peters, set designer; Ted Williams, book designer;
    Wanda Winch, photo researcher/photo editor

Photo Credits
AP/Wide World Photos/Thomas Grimm, 23
Capstone Press/Karon Dubke, front cover, 4, 6 (both), 7, 8, 26
Corbis/Bettmann, 20, 22, 24, 25
Courtesy of Larry C. Liebscher, www.ForensicHandwriting.com, 1, 12, 13, 14, 19
Getty Images Inc./David S. Holloway, 28; Stone/Leland Bobbe, 16; Time Life
    Pictures, 17
PhotoEdit Inc./David Young-Wolff, 10
Shutterstock, back cover; Alan Egginton, 27

**CEDAR-FOX program courtesy of the Center of Excellence for Document
Analysis and Recognition (CEDAR), University of Buffalo, State University of
New York**

**Capstone Press thanks Larry C. Liebscher, www.ForensicHandwriting.com, for his
assistance with this book.**

1 2 3 4 5 6 12 11 10 09 08 07

Table of Contents

Chapter 1:   A Bullet at Dinner 5

Chapter 2:   Questions of Identity.......................... 11

Chapter 3:   Clues on Paper 15

Chapter 4:   Tracing a Paper Trail 21

Glossary 30

Read More 31

Internet Sites.. 31

Index.. 32

CHAPTER 1

Learn about:
- An unknown enemy
- A list of suspects
- Writing samples

A Bullet at Dinner

David Hanson owned a small business in Madison, Wisconsin. One evening, he was eating dinner at home with his wife. Suddenly, their peaceful evening was interrupted by the sound of breaking glass. A bullet had rocketed through the dining room window. It crashed into a framed picture just above Hanson's head.

The Hansons ran into another room and called the police. When the police came, they asked Hanson if he had any enemies. At first, he could think of no one. Then Hanson's wife remembered some strange notes. They were left in the family's mailbox on two mornings during the past month.

◀ The Hansons were horrified when a bullet crashed through their window.

The text of the notes threatened harm to Hanson and his family. But the notes were so poorly written that Hanson thought they were a joke. He put them away and forgot about them.

The officers looked at the notes. They asked Hanson to make a list of anyone who might be angry with him. Then the officers collected writing samples from each person on the list.

The letters Hanson received threatened him and his family.

Time to Compare

The officers sent the samples to forensic document examiner Allen Blake. Blake compared the handwriting of each sample to the writing on the notes. The writer had tried to disguise the handwriting. But the letters "t" and "g" were formed in a unique way in both the sample and the notes.

In his lab, Blake used a microscope to compare the samples to the notes.

After studying the evidence, Blake said he believed a woman named Jane Mason wrote the notes. Mason once worked for Hanson, but Hanson had fired her several months before. Police then searched Mason's home. They found a handgun hidden in the basement. Tests proved it was the same gun that had fired the shot into Hanson's home.

Preventing a Murder

Police arrested Mason at her home. She was mentally ill. Her illness made her believe Hanson had ruined her life by firing her. The judge sent Mason to a hospital for treatment. In this case, the work of the document examiner probably saved a life. It helped police catch a dangerous person before she hurt or killed someone.

◄ After her arrest, Mason admitted writing the letters and firing the shot into Hanson's house.

CHAPTER 2

Learn about:
- Handwriting habits
- Tricks and traps
- Changes in handwriting

Questions of Identity

No two people have handwriting that is exactly alike. Most people learn to write in elementary school. By their late teens, they have developed their own way of writing.

Forensic document examiners can pick out strong similarities between two pieces of writing. They can show that a person likely wrote a particular note. That information can point police toward a new suspect. It can also help a jury decide if a suspect is guilty or not.

Patterns Don't Lie

Document examiners must examine writing samples closely. Criminals often try to disguise their handwriting. For example, they might write in tiny letters or large block letters. They might change their writing hand or slant their writing sharply to the left or right.

◀ Most people's handwriting patterns can be identified by the time they are out of high school.

People's handwriting can vary for other reasons. If a person uses alcohol or drugs, his or her handwriting may look different.

But no matter how much a person's handwriting varies, there are underlying patterns that are hard to hide. Those patterns are most easily seen in little habits. The way a person crosses a "t" or dots an "i" can be important. One person might form the letter "g" in a completely different way than another person does.

Even if the writer tries to disguise his or her writing, some things don't change.

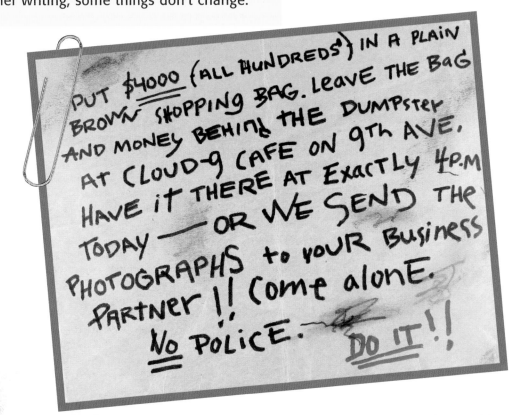

PUT $4000 (ALL HUNDREDS) IN A PLAIN BROWN SHOPPING BAG. LEAVE THE BAG AND MONEY BEHIND THE DUMPSTER AT CLOUD-9 CAFE ON 9Th AVE. HAVE it THERE AT EXACTLY 4P.M TODAY — OR WE SEND THE PHOTOGRAPHS to YOUR BUSINESS PARTNER !! COME ALONE. NO POLICE. DO IT !!

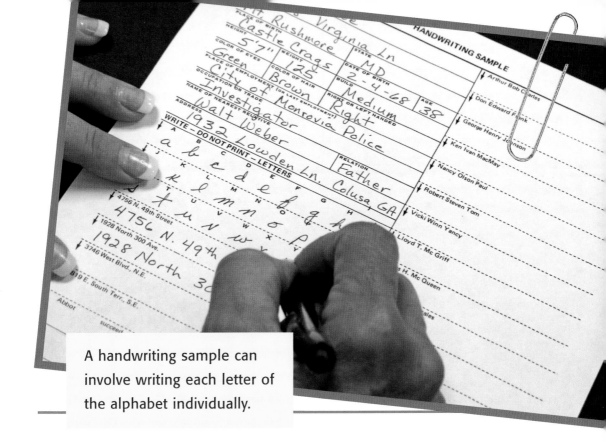

A handwriting sample can involve writing each letter of the alphabet individually.

Studying Samples

Document examiners pay close attention to the characteristics of handwriting. Each of these characteristics helps make a person's handwriting unique. That is why examiners like to study as many known documents as possible. The more samples there are, the easier it is to see a pattern of characteristics.

Suspects asked to provide samples may try to disguise how they write. But old habits are hard to change. The document examiner is trained to uncover any attempts at disguise. When enough samples have been gathered, the examiner is ready to go to work.

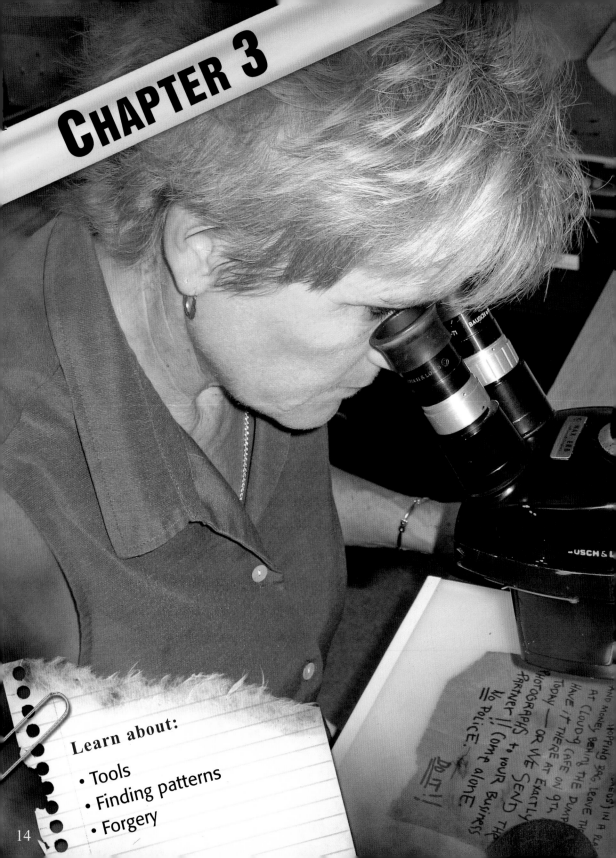

CHAPTER 3

Learn about:

- Tools
- Finding patterns
- Forgery

Clues on Paper

Much of a forensic document examiner's work involves paper. But they also work with any other surface people write on. These surfaces include dry erase boards, sidewalks, and even bathroom walls.

Basic tools examiners use include magnifying glasses and low-power microscopes. If examiners want to look closely at the ink used, they might shine an ultraviolet or infrared light on the sample. Then, they use a special viewer that filters out certain kinds of light. This can show if different types of ink were used. For example, a person might change a dollar amount or a date on a document.

◄ Document examiners use microscopes to study the details of a document.

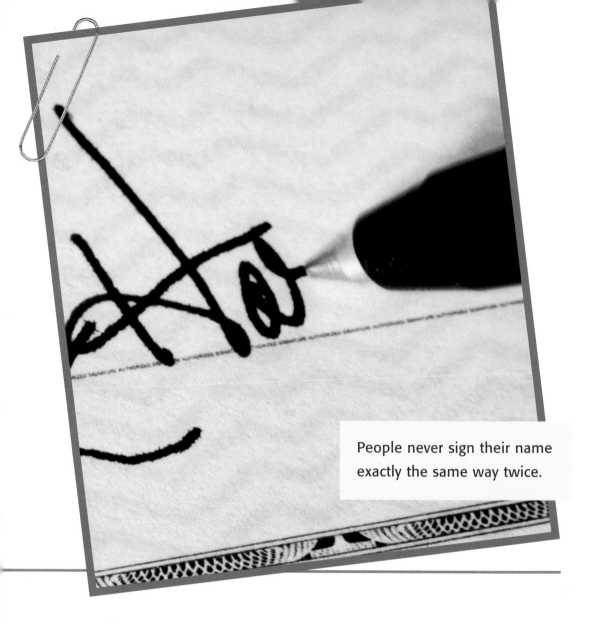

People never sign their name exactly the same way twice.

Searching for a Pattern

Much time is spent studying exactly how each letter is formed. The direction that the words slant is a clue. How hard the pen or pencil is pressed against the paper is another clue. Examiners also study the height of the letters and the spaces between them.

The goal is to find a person's natural writing pattern. The examiner then compares the pattern to the pattern used on a document associated with a crime. It might be a note given to a bank teller during a robbery. It could be a ransom note from a kidnapping. Or it might be a person's name on a check or legal document.

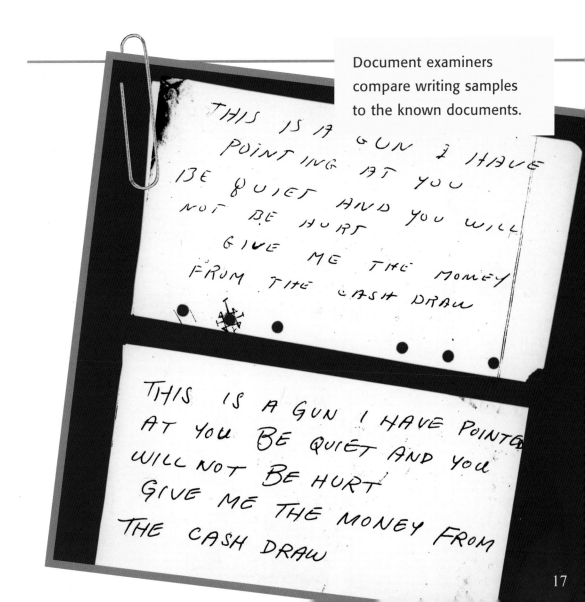

Document examiners compare writing samples to the known documents.

THIS IS A GUN I HAVE
POINTING AT YOU
BE QUIET AND YOU WILL
NOT BE HURT
GIVE ME THE MONEY
FROM THE CASH DRAW

THIS IS A GUN I HAVE POINTG
AT YOU BE QUIET AND YOU
WILL NOT BE HURT
GIVE ME THE MONEY FROM
THE CASH DRAW

Forgery Tricks

Signing someone else's name to a document with the intent of committing a crime is called forgery. It is easy to spot a forgery if the forger uses his or her own handwriting. It becomes harder when the forger tries to copy the other person's signature.

Forgers sometimes place a document with an actual signature on top of a document they want to forge. Next, they write firmly over the signature. They then use a pen to trace the indented signature.

A traced signature is easy for a document examiner to spot. Tracing a signature requires a different amount of pressure than most ordinary writing. The difference can be seen under a microscope or magnifying glass. Also, no one ever signs his or her name exactly the same way twice. If two signatures match perfectly, one probably has been forged.

Skilled forgers look at a person's signature and forge it by drawing it freehand. This type of forgery may be harder to uncover. When drawing freehand, the hand moves more naturally than it does when tracing.

A traced signature is easier to spot than a freehand copy. ➡

EXHIBIT 3-A

CENTRAL COAST HIGH SCHOOL
8TH Grade Annual Field Trip
Permission Slip

Known Signature (K1)

Permission is hereby given for JESSICA JEAN GLADSTONE to participate in the 8TH Grade's annual field trip to Lassen Canyon Park.

_____
Parent or Legal Guardian

Questioned Signature (Q1)

ACKNOWLEDGEMENT

Husband and Wife acknowledge that each has entered into all terms and conditions of this agreement without duress or undue influence.

Signed and dated this ___22___ day of ___JUNE___2006.

_____
Harold B. Gladstone

_____
Faye Gladstone

Q1

_____
Faye Gladstone

K1

_____
Parent or Legal Guardian

K1/Q1 Superimposition (Photoshop Elements 4.0)

_____
Faye Gladstone

19

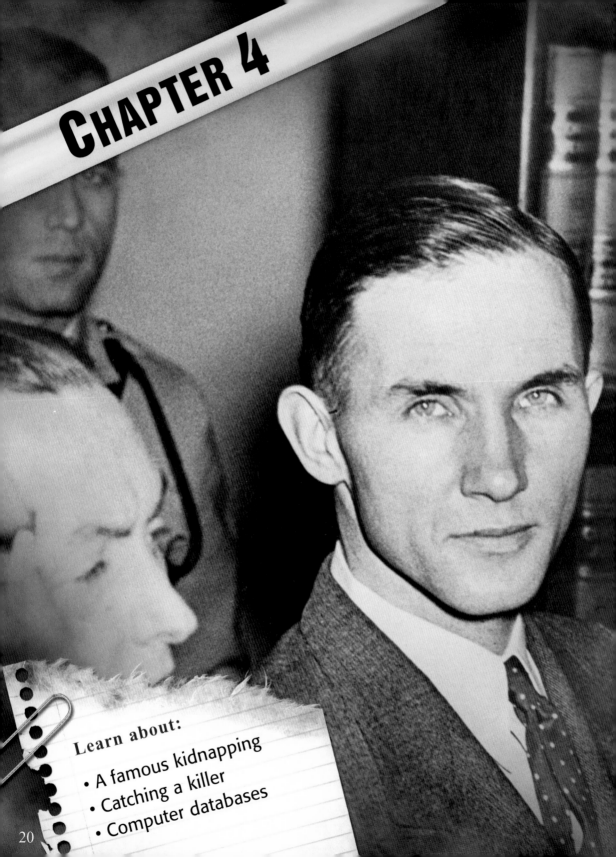

CHAPTER 4

Learn about:

- A famous kidnapping
- Catching a killer
- Computer databases

Tracing a Paper Trail

In the 1930s, document evidence helped convict one of the most famous criminals in U.S. history. Back then, Charles Lindbergh was a national hero. He was the first person to fly a plane across the Atlantic Ocean alone.

On March 1, 1932, Lindbergh's young son, Charles Jr., was taken from his home. A ransom note was left behind. The Lindberghs received other notes after the kidnapping. Although they paid the ransom, the child was found dead about two months later.

In 1934, police arrested Bruno Hauptmann. A gold certificate that was part of the ransom had been deposited in Hauptmann's bank account. Police found more ransom money in Hauptmann's garage. But more evidence was needed to convict him. Document examiners compared Hauptmann's writing with the ransom notes.

◄ Hauptmann insisted that he didn't kidnap the Lindbergh baby.

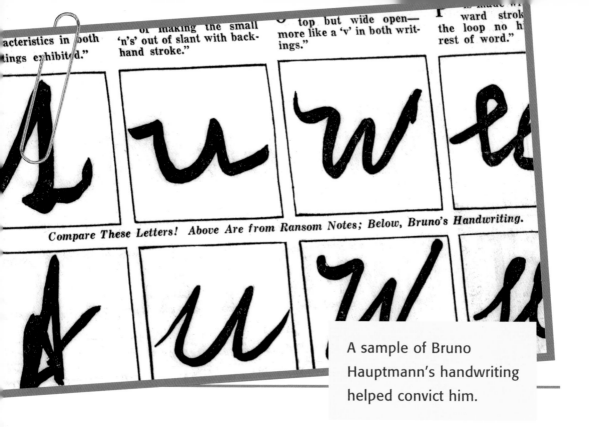

acteristics in both
tings exhibited."

or making the small
'n's' out of slant with back-
hand stroke."

top but wide open—
more like a 'v' in both writ-
ings."

ward strok
the loop no h
rest of word."

Compare These Letters! Above Are from Ransom Notes; Below, Bruno's Handwriting.

A sample of Bruno Hauptmann's handwriting helped convict him.

Hauptmann's writing samples had many unusual characteristics. He wrote the word "to" as if it were a "w." He also had a strange way of writing the word "the." These habits and others were also in the ransom note. The examiners concluded that Hauptmann wrote the notes. Their findings and the other evidence led the jury to convict Hauptmann.

Hitler Diaries

In 1983, publishers of the German magazine *Stern* thought they had made a major discovery. A man named Konrad Kujau claimed to have 62 diaries written by former

German dictator Adolf Hitler. The publishers paid Kujau a large sum of money for the diaries.

The publishers believed the diaries were real. But many other people did not. The German government asked document examiners to review the diaries. The examiners found that the paper contained materials not used before 1950. Hitler died in 1945. Also, the handwriting didn't match Hitler's. Kujau then confessed to writing the diaries himself. He was sent to prison for his crime.

Stern magazine planned to publish the Hitler diaries.

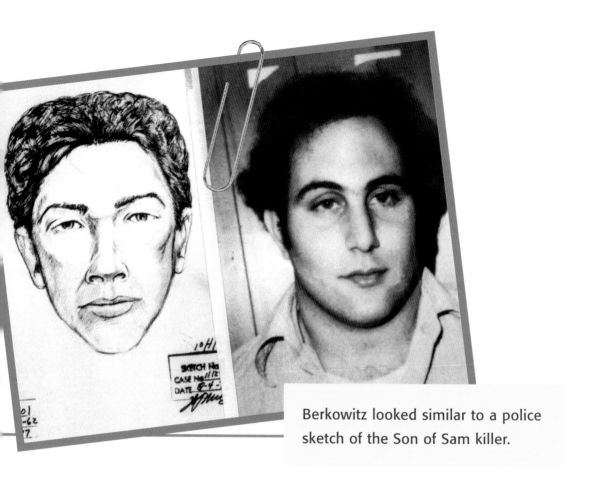

Berkowitz looked similar to a police sketch of the Son of Sam killer.

Son of Sam

Another famous case involved a killer in the late 1970s. The killer called himself the Son of Sam in letters he sent to the police.

The killer shot 13 people in New York City. The victims were out walking or sitting in their cars. Six of them died. Notes were found at some of the crime scenes.

After a shooting in July 1977, a witness saw a car speeding away from the scene. The car had a parking ticket on the windshield. Police checked their records for parking tickets written on that street that night. They learned the car belonged to David Berkowitz. When police searched the car, a gun and a note were inside. The gun was the one used in the shootings. The handwriting matched the notes and letters the police received. Berkowitz was convicted and sent to prison for life.

Berkowitz sent threatening letters to his neighbor, Deputy Sheriff Craig Glassman.

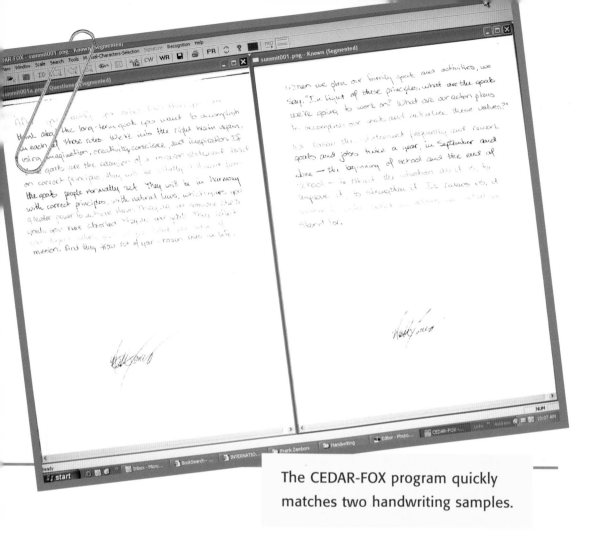

The CEDAR-FOX program quickly matches two handwriting samples.

FOX and FISH

Today, document examiners use computers in exciting new ways. Researchers at the University of Buffalo in New York developed a program called CEDAR-FOX. The program was developed for the U.S. Postal Service to read handwritten addresses on envelopes. By the late 1990s, forensic document examiners were also using CEDAR-FOX.

Using CEDAR-FOX, computers can usually recognize whether two samples of handwriting are from the same person. The process is called optical handwriting recognition (OHR). If the handwriting sample of the suspect is in the database, the program can save months of work. This is especially true if investigators have to examine thousands of documents.

A Deadly Gift

Forensic document evidence helped solve a case in 1922 in Marshfield, Wisconsin. James Chapman got a package in the mail. When his wife opened the package, it blew up. She was killed, and Chapman was badly hurt.

Police pieced together scraps of paper from the package. They found enough to read the address line. The writer misspelled Marshfield as "Marsfilld." This spelling made police think the writer might be Swedish. Interviewing Swedish people near Marshfield led police to John Magnuson. Magnuson and Chapman were bitter enemies.

Police collected writing samples from Magnuson. They matched the writing and spelling on the package. At Magnuson's farm, police found bomb-making materials and an ink bottle containing the same ink that was on the package. Magnuson was convicted and sent to prison for life.

The U.S. Secret Service is another group that uses computers to help investigators identify handwriting. The Secret Service's job is to protect the president and other top government officials.

Their computer program is called the Forensic Information System for Handwriting (FISH). The program changes handwriting samples into computer files. The computer then can automatically compare a sample with about 100,000 other handwriting samples in the Secret Service database. The computer is much faster at comparing samples than a person is.

Computer technology gives document examiners a big advantage in solving document mysteries. That is not good news for kidnappers, forgers, and other criminals. Document examiners plan to continue using advances in technology to help police solve crimes.

◄ Secret Service agents protect top government officials.

Glossary

characteristic (ka-rik-tuh-RISS-tik)—a typical quality or feature

disguise (diss-GIZE)—to hide something

infrared light (IN-fruh-red LITE)—light that produces heat; people cannot see infrared light.

optical (OP-tuh-kuhl)—of or relating to sight

ransom (RAN-suhm)—money that is demanded before someone who is being held captive can be set free

recognition (rek-uhg-NI-shuhn)—the act of becoming aware that something is true or correct or has been seen before

signature (SIG-nuh-chur)—the individual way that a person writes his or her name

suspect (SUHSS-pekt)—a person believed to be responsible for a crime

ultraviolet light (uhl-truh-VYE-uh-lit LITE)—invisible light rays; the sun produces ultraviolet light.

Read More

Bauchner, Elizabeth. *Document Analysis*. Forensics: The Science of Crime-Solving. Philadelphia: Mason Crest, 2006.

Rainis, Kenneth G. *Forgery: Crime-Solving Science Experiments*. Forensic Science Projects. Berkeley Heights, N.J.: Enslow, 2006.

Stewart, Gail B. *Forgery*. Crime Scene Investigations. Detroit: Lucent Books, 2007.

Internet Sites

FactHound offers a safe, fun way to find Internet sites related to this book. All of the sites on FactHound have been researched by our staff.

Here's how:

1. Visit *www.facthound.com*

2. Choose your grade level.

3. Type in this book ID **0736867880** for age-appropriate sites. You may also browse subjects by clicking on letters, or by clicking on pictures and words.

4. Click on the **Fetch It** button.

FactHound will fetch the best sites for you!

Index

cases
    Hitler diaries, 23
    Lindbergh kidnapping,
     21, 22
    Marshfield bombing, 27
    Son of Sam, 24–25
CEDAR-FOX, 26–27
computers, 26–27, 29

equipment
    infrared lights, 15
    magnifying glasses, 15, 18
    microscopes, 7, 15, 18
    ultraviolet lights, 15

FISH, 29
forgery, 18, 29

handwriting
    characteristics, 13, 22
    disguises, 7, 11, 12, 13
    patterns, 11, 12, 13, 17
    samples, 6, 7, 11, 13, 15,
     17, 22, 26, 27, 29

ink, 15, 27
investigators, 27, 29

optical handwriting recognition
    (OHR), 27

signatures, 18
suspects, 11, 13, 27

writing surfaces, 15